The Tiger, the Man and the Jackal

A Folktale from India

retold by **Lee S. Justice**
illustrated by **Krystyna Stasiak**

HOUGHTON MIFFLIN   BOSTON

Once upon a time, a tiger was trapped in a cage. The tiger tried to squeeze out. But the bars were too close together.

The tiger tried to bite through the bars. But the bars were too hard.

The tiger shook the bars. He hit them. But it was no use. He could not get out.

A man came strolling by the cage.
"Please, let me out!" cried the tiger.
"I cannot help you," said the man. "If I let you out, you would eat me."

"No, I would never eat you!" promised the tiger. "Please free me. I will be your servant for the rest of your days!"

The tiger cried and begged. The man listened. He felt sorry for the tiger.

The man opened the door to the cage.

The tiger leaped out. He did not say thank
you. Instead he said, "You look delicious." The
man turned and ran.

After a short chase, the tiger pounced on the man. "I am famished," said the tiger. "Now I will eat you."

"Wait, wait!" cried the man. "You are not being fair!"

"Yes, I am fair," said the tiger.

"Not fair," said the man.

"Fair," said the tiger.

A jackal came strolling by. He stopped to listen.

"Let's ask the jackal if you are being fair," said the man. "Let the jackal decide if I will be your meal."

The tiger agreed. "I will go along with what the jackal decides," said the tiger.

The man told the jackal what had happened. The jackal listened.

The jackal scratched his head. "I'm mixed up," he said. "Would you mind telling me the whole story again?"

The man told the story again.

The jackal frowned. "I still do not understand," he said. "Show me where this took place. Maybe then I will be able to figure out what happened."

The tiger, the man, and the jackal went back to the cage. The man began to tell the story again.

The jackal said, "This is all so mixed up in my head. You were in the cage, and the tiger came strolling by?"

"No, no!" the tiger said. "I was in the cage, and the man came strolling by."

"Oh, now I understand," said the jackal. "I was in the cage. No, that can't be right. The cage was in the tiger. No, that's not right either. Let me see. The man must have been in the tiger, and the cage came walking by."

The tiger grew more and more angry. "Look here, foolish jackal!" he cried. "*I* am the tiger. *He* is the man. *That* is the cage. *I* was in the cage!"

"But I still don't understand," said the jackal. "How did you get in the cage?"

The tiger could not control his rage. He
jumped into the cage and shouted, "I was in the
cage. Like this! Now do you understand?"

"Yes, I understand," answered the jackal calmly. Then he locked the cage door.

The jackal turned to the man. "Now, let us leave things as they were," said the jackal with a smile. And they walked off together.